*You Hue: Fun meeting you –*

# THE
# BUMPEDY ROAD

## A True
## International
## Adventure

*Be blessed,*

### by Kiska, the Cat

*(as told to Pamela Bauer Mueller)*

*Pamela Bauer Mueller*

*09/09/2022*

PIÑATA PUBLISHING

Copyright © 1999 Pamela Bauer Mueller
Second printing: 2000
Third printing: 2001
Fourth printing: 2004
Fifth printing: 2006
Sixth printing: 2011
Seventh printing: 2018

All rights reserved. No part of this book may be reproduced in any form or by any means without permission by the publisher. Reviewers and critics may, however, quote short passages.

Piñata Publishing
626 Old Plantation Road
Jekyll Island, GA 31527
(912) 635-9402

www.pinatapub.com

CANADIAN CATALOGUING IN PUBLICATION
Mueller, Pamela Bauer
   The bumpedy road

ISBN: 978-0-9685097-0-8

   1. Cats—Juvenile fiction. I. Title.
PZ7.M869BU 1999   J813'.54   C99-910514-0

Library of Congress Card Number: 00-131963

Typeset by Vancouver Desktop Publishing Centre
Printed and bound in the United States by Patterson Printing

I dedicate this book to my parents,
Phyllis and Don,
who encouraged me
to believe in myself
and trust in Him.

*Also by Pamela Bauer Mueller*

## The Kiska Trilogy

The Bumpedy Road
Rain City Cats
Eight Paws to Georgia


## The Aloha Set

Hello, Goodbye, I Love You
Aloha Crossing


## Historical Novels

Neptune's Honor
An Angry Drum Echoed
Splendid Isolation

# Acknowledgements

I wish to gratefully acknowledge the following people who instructed, supported and guided me in the writing of "The Bumpedy Road."

Georgeanne Irvine, for inspiration and for being my role model.

Mimi Cummings, for providing your sunny home to get me started.

Pamela Pollack, for teaching me to focus, and making my characters more fun.

Carolyn and David Foltz, for sharing your publishing and marketing skills.

Gary Page, for working with me on computer techniques.

Cassandra and Ticiana, my daughters, for the pictures and fond memories.

Naomi Weiler, for your enthusiasm and contagious energy.

Patty Osborne, for making book publication fun.

Michael, my husband, (whose creative input resulted in the cover design) thank you for your encouragement, patience, loving criticism and for believing we could.

# Prologue

This story of my life is based on actual events. However, there may be moments where I have altered or decorated the facts just a bit whenever they could have reflected unfavorably on me. And, being a cat, I retain the rights to my privacy whenever desired.

If you wish to learn about cats, only a cat can tell you. Humans mean well when they write cat stories, but they are far less advanced than they fancy themselves. Sometimes, but rarely, a human is lucky enough to imagine part of himself into a cat. This would allow that person's cat to imagine part of himself into a human being. And that's where the magical relationship begins! I am one of those lucky cats.

I was born in Mexico City, lived out my young years there, then moved to San Diego, California as a young adult. Both my brother, Canica, and I are bilingual and bicultural. We are equally comfortable being summoned with "bichu bichu" by our Mexican maid or "kitty, kitty, here kitty" in English. Because of this, we have perfected the art of eavesdropping to our great advantage, allowing us to be the architects of our own lives.

This journal follows my humble birth in Mexico City, my carefree childhood and youth, and a portion of my adult years in California. It will take you on an adventurous roller coaster ride of stories—some happy, some sad, others frightening and challenging, but all meaningful. This unique and interesting tale depicts only a part of my life. Even as you read this page, I'm sunning myself and dreaming of the sequel.

# Contents

# My First Birthday Party

I suppose my first birthday party would be the day of my birth, if one were to be totally accurate. To be honest, I don't remember that day, but I'm sure it was a party of sorts. I was told that I was the seventh kitten born in my litter that warm September afternoon, and that I was the "runt." This, of course, accounts for my petite size and high intelligence, so the Mistress says, but I am digressing.

What I do remember is being hungry. My siblings had a head start in learning the knack of survival, as I was always being pushed away, uprooted and disjoined from my mother's teats. She would eventually nudge me back in and warm me up, at the same time washing and attending the other six. I had one sister and all the rest were male kittens, so we quickly learned competitive skills.

My first memories are about the time my eyes opened and I began to observe my surroundings. My mother loomed big and beautiful before me, and I immediately understood that she was my boss. My father was never introduced to us; Mom did not even mention him, and we were too young to know we had one. We merrily went about our business of learning to walk, falling, playing, nipping at each other, and especially eating. Just when we became quite proficient at nursing, Mom began to disappear for periods of time, and leave us to our own diversions. That's when I discovered that each one of us has a personality.

Two of my brothers loved to box, so my sister and I were used for warm up purposes before their matches. Another sibling taught us how to tumble and roll down the hill, so we conducted races and bet on the results. Being so tiny, I was quick and often won. One afternoon, my youngest brother found a wild iguana, which spat at us and sent us all running. I learned to distinguish my brothers and sister by their traits and noises rather than by their looks. I guess cats don't dwell on markings or colors (we barely discern colors) to recognize each other because they know one's presence through sounds and smells.

So Mother introduced us to life and we frolicked through our carefree first weeks. There was a small fence separating our house from the neighbors', and we scrambled up and over it about the fourth week. One afternoon we heard children laughing and shouting beyond that fence, and smelled the wonderful aromas of barbequed chicken. Several of my brothers clambered up the fence, where they sat spellbound. The children had a long stick and were beating on a suspended colorful donkey, made of paper mache and pottery. Candies, oranges and peanuts were spilling from it everywhere. My brothers shouted for us to join them, and we watched in amazement as the children playfully pushed, screamed and fought their ways to the treats tumbling to the ground. We were able to observe this "piñata party" tradition many more times, and never did understand why the adults insisted that the small children beat the beautiful figures until they broke.

My first contact with the owners of the back yard where we lived was about five days into my first week. I smelled an unusual presence approaching, but was nursing and safe, so paid no heed. The lady of the house petted each of us and spoke softly and sweetly to our mother. My sense was that this was an additional part of our day's activities. Strangely, I did not see this lady again for almost three weeks, and by then I'd forgotten her. Looking back, I believe she did not want to become too attached to us. Nevertheless, when she reappeared and tried to pick us up, we all scattered, more from instinct than fear. Our mother was away, so we had no guidance, and I followed my siblings, as I did in most things. Later, Mother assured us that the owners were indeed our friends, but the doubt remained.

We grew and discovered our surroundings, spending the first six weeks of our lives totally unmindful of a world beyond our back yard. Mother weaned us and soft food began appearing, which we devoured with ravenous appetites. We still tried to nurse, but Mother had enough. She taught us to chase little creatures, refereed our spats, insisted on personal cleanliness, and showed us feline etiquette. The boys often interrupted our washing sessions by darting off to chase earthworms or bugs, and Mom patiently brought them back to class.

One afternoon we noticed a bowl of cool tasteless white liquid next to our soft food. Instead of warm rich milk from our mom, we were offered cool pasteurized cows' milk, which we eventually learned to drink. This should have been a clue as to the changes that were to come. But I, at least, was oblivious, and enjoyed my life to the fullest.

# Adoption

**W**hen I was six weeks old, people began arriving at our back yard. We had no idea why they were there, but their voices startled us and even our mother was flustered. Perhaps this had happened in the past, or her intuition alerted her. When they approached and reached for us, we dodged their grasps and ran off in many directions to hide. These people were noisy, and had a mission. The mission was to capture a kitten or two, which we quickly comprehended. Sometimes several of us were caught, and the interested parties would turn us over and make us mew in protest. I made it a point to loudly voice my indignation, which seemed to work, because I was released and left alone. The first time strange people came to see us nobody was selected, and we all resumed our peaceful living.

Several days later, a man and a woman came outside to see us. They were soft spoken and seemed quiet. After quite a struggle, the lady of the house picked up two of my brothers and handed them to the couple, who quickly deposited them in a basket and left! We were shocked and frightened. Perhaps we sensed we would never see them again. After crying softly for several hours, my siblings and I finally fell into an exhausted slumber. I feel certain that our mother mourned them for some time. This was my introduction to the ways of the human world. No longer were we safe in our haven.

But, as kittens have short memories, we were pretty much back to normal the following morning. As the week unfolded, we had accepted the fact that our brothers were gone, and so we concentrated on frolicking in the fields out behind our property and reveling in the lovely late autumn days. There were trees to climb, and we learned which ones made excellent scratching posts. My sister tried filing her claws on a cactus plant one afternoon, and her howl sent us all running. There she sat, looking puzzled and pitiful, shaking her paw back and forth. Mother was finally able to remove the thorn from her foot by pulling it out with her teeth. Another lesson was learned.

By now we were all quite independent, and the boys were downright rowdy. They had progressed from boxing to tackle football, a game my sister and I refused to join. We girls were more delicate, and I was still the smallest, but we each held our own. None of us had names, of course, but we addressed each other by signals and mews, and managed very well among ourselves. We also devised a vocabulary of coded words, very similar to secret languages that children invent.

One afternoon, because of this coded warning signal, I became aware that more humans were approaching. As we ran for shelter, I noticed that the lady of the house was accompanied by another lady and two young girls. What happened next still surprises me. Suddenly these children took off after us, running and laughing through the back yard, working themselves up into quite a tizzy. We must have been hissing and growling, because the lady of the house went off to fetch heavy gloves. She finally succeeded in capturing both me and my largest and strongest brother! He was most upset, and put up quite a fight, so I followed suit. The children, however, seemed pleased with the selection, and the two women discussed details of our caring. We were then placed in a cardboard box and boarded up. The box was set in the back seat of an automobile, and we were driven to our new home.

On our ride home, we were introduced to human conversation, with its intonations and unusually loud sounding decibels. Perhaps everyone was just excited, but we yelped and scratched and protested with kitten howls. Festive Mexican mariachi music blared from the radio. When we reached the house, we were carried, still in the box, to a room in the back which adjoined the kitchen. After the Mistress had set up our food dishes and bathroom facilities, we were released. The two little girls wanted to stay and observe us, but were lead away so that we could become accustomed to our surroundings. As evening fell, my brother and I settled down and actually relaxed enough to fall into a fitful sleep. I dreamed of Mother, of our siblings, and of warm snuggling. Thankfully, I remembered I was curled up beside my big brother. Cuddled together, we slept, and awoke to our first day in our new home.

# The Adoptive Family

Before going further, I should describe myself. Both my brother and I are tabby cats. We are a mixture of brown, grey, and white and have broad black stripes on our backs. I've heard us referred to as "alley cats," and I take that as a compliment, for I've known many handsome alley cats. My Master described us as a "European domestic" breed. In any event, we have the nicest soft teddy bearish brown and white fur on our tummies, which we love having brushed. And that is how the children, Miss Cassandra and Miss Ticiana, found their ways into our hearts.

Upon awakening the following morning, my brother and I took quick inventory of our new home. Instead of sleeping in the outdoors, nestled next to several warm bodies, I found myself inside a rag filled box in a warm room, cuddling with my brother. There were dishes on the floor containing rich milk and a wonderful concoction of rice and sardines. From the kitchen came aromas of breakfast being cooked, and morning greetings were being exchanged by my new masters. The children were dressed in pajamas, and eagerly waiting to "tame us." Let me describe my adoptive family to you.

The Master of the house was an architect and spent a lot of time away from the house. He was a "converted" cat person, meaning that, although he always liked cats, he learned the importance of communicating with us through the Mistress. He had a warm body to lie on, and encouraged us to meet him each evening when he pulled into the carport.

The Mistress was a true cat person, recognizing that my brother and I are the real "masters" of the household. She has always been owned by cats and has taught everyone around her to respect our dignity. Most of the time she was around, but her career sometimes took her away for weeks, and then we truly missed her. After a while we learned that she moved here from the United States to marry the Master. Good fortune for us!

The oldest child, Miss Cassandra, was eleven when we met and, like her mom, knew how to communicate with us from the start. On that first morning, she crouched down so that our faces were more or less on the same level. This is how she chose to communicate on an equal basis. She spoke softly to us without cooing or patronizing, and I took an immediate liking to her. She also gave me my innovative name, but more on that in another chapter.

Little Miss Ticiana was still a child when we met,

eight years old, but respectful and understanding of our needs and wishes. She had a very playful nature and a happy-go-lucky personality, and could be depended on to heed our every wish with minimal communication. Fortunately, both of these children were mature enough to have outgrown any annoying traits, like chasing after us or pulling our tails.

So, with a little inbred suspicion and a hopeful heart I waited for these people to find us. Just a few minutes passed before two little faces were peeking at us from behind the door, and one moment later, they each had one of us in their arms. Of course we squirmed and meowed a bit, but it was mostly a front, for we knew adoration and devotion when we saw it.

After breakfast the Mistress brought forth a hairbrush, and put my brother and me on her lap tummy side up. She ran the brush through our fur and then passed me to Miss Cassandra, who finished up the grooming. My brother, who was not so sure he liked this idea, was handled by both the Mistress and Miss Ticiana. I later heard them say that we were quite wild for several days, but my memory is that after this brushing session, we became tame.

There was another member of our household whom I must mention here: Señorita Teresa, who lived with us and worked as a full time housekeeper. She had a cheerful disposition and learned to anticipate our every need. After listening to the Mistress call us by "here kitty, kitty," Teresa wanted to imitate her and do the same. The other Spanish speaking maids living in our compound found that so amusing that sometimes they would mimic her, so we eventually explored all of the houses up there on the hill.

Our house was one of eight situated in a beautiful tree lined compound above Mexico City in the town of Contadero. The Master's mother described the landscaping as similar to the Gardens of Versailles in France, but I wouldn't know anything about France. Directly behind our house was a forest, which provided constant exploration, as we quickly became indoor/outdoor cats. Our front lawn connected with everyone else', so there were several acres of flowers, trees, plants, forts and swing sets, complete with all the small critters that those attract. At the entrance of our compound was a chicken farm, awarding my brother and me hours of reckless pleasure scaring the fearful old hens and chasing after the chicks.

In the late afternoons, we would often hide behind the plants until the caretaker closed up the chicken coop for the night. Then we crawled on our tummies to the coop, very quietly so that the hens and baby chicks were not aware of our arrival. With a leap and a meow, we jumped up onto the window sill and began to stalk them from above. Finally, we squeezed, one at a time, through a tiny tear in the screen, and slowly worked our way down the wall. This was difficult, especially when we were small, and the height frightened us. But soon we jumped to the ground, and the fun began.

We just had to walk about through the pens to cause a commotion. The peeping chickens scattered everywhere, the hens squawked noisily and danced about, their feathers flying! What fun we had upsetting their peaceful world. Sometimes we would chase a baby chick, carefully avoiding the hens who would peck us if they could. We never really wanted to

catch the chicks, just play the game. Once, a care-taker was in the back room and discovered our game. He swatted us and tossed us out the back door. We returned a few days later, and continued to enjoy our pastime. Our living situation was truly idyllic.

Now let us move forward to begin recalling the adventures of my childhood.

# The Naming Game

On Sunday, my new family gave us names. I felt no lack of self esteem without one, since I didn't know I needed one. But as the family was discussing possibilities, the thought of having an official title became appealing to me. Somewhere in the midst of the discussion the question of length came up. The adults wanted a single syllable, more practical for calling us. The children wanted long titles, because they were more fun to invent. Each child was allowed to name a cat. I think that was the moment that Miss Cassandra chose me and Miss Ticiana got my brother.

As it turned out, my name has two syllables and is short and serviceable. It is also very pleasing to the ear, and feminine. After the Mistress offered several suggestions, Miss Cassandra chose the name "Kiska," which means "cat" in Russian.

Names last a lifetime and often mistakes are made with humorous intention. This was not the case in my brother's name, however. If his name sounds amusing to you, it was simply coincidental. Miss Ticiana thought for a very long time, rejecting all suggestions from the others. Finally, Miss Cassandra became exasperated, and an idea popped into Miss Ticiana's head. She might have been playing with marbles at the time. I don't know because my brother and I had fallen asleep in the patch of sunshine on the living room floor. We were awakened by a loud "Canica, that's it," shouted by Miss Ticiana (in Spanish, because that was her preferred language at that time.) In Spanish masculine names often end in an "o," denoting male gender, and this was pointed out to Miss Ticiana. But she had made her choice, and "Canica" it was. That word means "marble" in Spanish, and neither Canica nor I saw the resemblance, but he accepted it gladly, as one does when new things are offered. We were learning that people are unpredictable.

Although Canica and I are both tabby cats and quite similar in coloring, we are actually quite distinct. From the tilt of our whiskers to the set of our ears and down to the shape of our tails, we are clearly differentiated. But most humans do not see beyond our basic markings, so the selection of our names dignified us. As we would soon discover, humans also confused our names, or simply resorted to acknowledging us as "nice kitty."

Armed with the prestige of our new names, we set out to relay this news to the other members of the animal kingdom. The neighboring cats quickly learned and respected our names, as we did theirs. Only a few of the dogs became friendly enough for us to exchange pleasantries with, and the birds just didn't care. (Nor did they come close enough for small talk.) Now we were ready to take on the world!

# Communicating
# With a Cat

Canica and I were allowed to explore outside very soon after we arrived. Our owners taught us how to use a litter box, and then, convinced that we understood the concept, removed it. From then on, the box would appear at night only. We were encouraged to spend time outside, at first in the fenced back patio, and then allowed to venture where we chose. Evidently our masters had experience with cats, recognized us as quick learners, and understood our need for adventure.

One day during our explorations, we came upon a neighbor's small basset hound dog. Having never encountered a dog up close, we bounded up to him with curiosity and delight. The hound crouched even lower to the ground than he already stood, growled and bared his teeth. Surprised and insulted by such treatment, we hissed and quickly retreated. That was our first attempt at canine interaction. Since then we've met many a dog that we disliked, a few who were tolerable, and even made some friends in that department.

Cats are students of behavior. We observe, note, and absorb. Sometimes we become hermit-like in our environment and somewhat suspicious of outsiders. When friends of the Master and Mistress come to visit, I judge them quickly by the way they communicate with me. If they speak intelligently, crouch low to see me on my level, and extend a hand before gathering me into their arms, I am quite receptive to their interest. However, if they make those ridiculous sounds that they think are pleasing to the feline ear, I am cautious and unimpressed. You know those sounds, the ones they make to babies: cooing, soothing, slightly high pitched murmurs. Cats truly appreciate humans who have a desire to communicate on an equal basis. Miss Cassandra and Miss Ticiana talk to us like friends, sharing stories about their day at school. They encourage us to listen to their phone conversations by holding us on their laps while they talk. When our names are mentioned, we perk up and feel honored. Often the adults in the household will share informational tidbits with us, always speaking to us on their level. Intelligent conversation is required for a cat to become smarter.

Although we do speak to each other and to other animals, cats have no need to talk to humans. Why should we talk when we can communicate without words? We can resort to pantomime to make our needs known. I make my wishes perfectly clear to anyone with powers of observation. I sniff to indicate suspicion or curiosity. I scratch objects to call your attention. I show my teeth to express disapproval. I rub against your ankle when I want service. And when I'm content, you'll know by my fixed and loving gaze, my vibrating purr, and my tremors of pleasure.

All cats have their own ways of showing enthusiasm and contentment. I will spread my toes wide open, making what my family calls "starfish paws." Then I will "make tortillas" with my nails on my chosen human's available arm, leg, or stomach. After all, I am a Mexican "gatita" (little kitty) so this manner of kneading, or "making tortillas" is very appropriate. And when I am extremely pleased with myself, I will prance, the tip of my tail carried straight up like a proud flag. By the same token, I may decide to ignore you. When called, I do not move a muscle. I will act as if I hadn't heard a thing. Sudden selective deafness is a common feline disorder. This is usually my reaction with very small children. I know their intention is to grab me, hoist me into their arms, and walk around with me, folded into a doll-like position. I hope that by not acknowledging them, they will forget about me and find a new interest.

If I discover a plateful of food which I consider unappetizing, I may approach the food in slow motion, sniff it, walk around it as if to understand its purpose, and look at the Mistress in silent displeasure. I will then shake each front paw in a gesture of scorn, attempt to bury this glob, and walk away. A cat must exert his will by refusing to eat until his master remembers that he requires top quality. In order to understand a cat, you must be observant.

# Rabbitsville

**M**y life in Mexico with my masters and their children was filled with adventures and exciting happenings. Canica and I had the run of the house and basically, the run of the compound, because we were young and reckless. During sunny mornings, we often made our way to each of the neighbor's homes, starting next door. The maids would welcome us inside, and discover some tasty morsel for us. Then we would explore their house, top to bottom. Around midmorning, we might curl up on a sunny window sill in a room above the kitchen, enjoying the delicious aromas of food cooking below.

Two houses down lived an older grey and white cat, named Bebe. She led us on many rodent chases, took us to the top of the birch tree, and introduced us to the chicken farm. From Bebe we learned the art of "schmoozing." She introduced us to the maids in every house in the compound. Watching her rub against their legs, lick their fingers and purr loudly in their ears, we practiced what we observed and soon became favorites along with Bebe. As time went by, these same maids would save chicken livers, cow brains and other delicacies for the three of us. One day we were able to repay Bebe the favor. On a lazy summer afternoon as she was walking the fence, her long fur caught in a piece of barbed wire. She yowled in pain, which awakened us from our nap on the windowsill. Canica and I rushed to her and rescued her, pulling out great tufts of her hair until she was freed.

The dogs living in the other houses proved to be lesser than we, as we had suspected from the beginning. We teased them mercilessly, usually two against one, and tormented them whenever we could. Two large boxers lived up the hill. Canica would dash up to them, and then zigzag back and forth confusing them as to which way to run. I would then circle around them or rush between their legs. This was quite a thrill for us, because they never got it. When chased, we escaped up the tree trunks.

Miss Cassandra and Miss Ticiana were tomboys, and we loved to join them when they played outdoors. On cool afternoon, they would wrap us up in wool serapes (shawls) and swing with us, going higher and faster until we all got dizzy. When they released us, we'd scatter and hide, but only until they began another activity. We joined them in hide and seek, showing them hiding places of our own. Sometimes we led

them to discover the other children's hide outs, but we had to stop when those children objected. We drew the line when Miss Ticiana wanted to jump with us on the trampoline.

I wonder if ever there were kittens living with little girls who were not dressed in doll clothes. It is a most annoying custom, but as I understand it, a common one for children twelve or under. On such occasions, we were picked up and carried into the bedroom or den, confined behind closed doors with little hope of escape. Then Miss Cassandra and Miss Ticiana would come forth with various articles of doll clothing, draping dresses over our heads and shoving our front feet through the sleeves. The worse part of it was trying to push our back legs into the doll's trousers. Mexico's numerous states have different native costumes, and I think these girls had them all. Imagine getting stuffed into the many layers of the Oaxacan or Chiapas regional dresses! Naturally, we voiced our concerns, but were kissed and coddled, and the clothes went on anyway. Both of us were relieved when the girls outgrew this pesky practice.

For over a year we were the only pets, and extremely spoiled. We grew almost plump on a diet of rice, chicken broth and sardines, which Señorita Teresa decided was proper cat food. The Mistress had checked out the local dry cat food sold at that time in Mexico, and thankfully, decided that it was inappropriate for us. As a variant, we were given scraps from the dinner table, and the young ladies gave us whatever they thought we would gobble up. Looking back, I decided that we were fed the tastiest variety and most delicious food during our years in Mexico. There were a few mistakes as well. Maybe the girls thought we would actually enjoy chili sauce on our tacos?

Sometime around our second Christmas with the family, the Mistress and Master thought it would be great fun to give their daughters rabbits for Christmas. They were told that the two rabbits they selected were females, so they tied pink bows around their necks and put them under the Christmas tree. Of course the girls were ecstatic with their new pets, and I must admit that Canica and I were jealous. Certainly we did not understand the euphoria over a couple of such limited creatures, so we opted to ignore them totally.

As time went by, it became evident that one of the rabbits was male, and a whole family of rabbits sprang forth. There must have been nine baby rabbits in the first batch, and everyone in the household, excluding the cats, was excited. The rabbits were now living in the laundry room, which was once our domain, while we had the roam of the house. But after this first litter of baby rabbits, the entire clan was moved to the outdoor patio. The Master then fenced in the whole area, and from that day on, more and more rabbits were born into the family. The Mistress returned from one of her visits to the United States with rabbit leashes, so the adult rabbits were walked about the compound by the three females in the family. That was truly a sight to behold!

I honestly do not understand why Señorita Teresa did not go on strike, as she ended up cleaning, sweeping, and feeding this menagerie. What began as Miss Cassandra's and Miss Ticiana's Christmas presents had become a tribe of thirty-two rabbits!

Early one morning we were rudely awakened by shouts from the Mistress that the fence had a hole and some of the rabbits had escaped! She was so upset that the Master went running behind the house in his pajamas in search of the escaped rabbits. Canica and I found this performance quite amusing and much more satisfying than any chasing that we could have done. To his credit, the Master rounded up about six baby rabbits and one adult, which he handed over to the distraught Mistress. Soon after that, the Master found an excellent farm home for all the rabbits.

# Valle De Bravo
# and the
# Bumpedy Road

Our family had a weekend home in a mountain town called Valle de Bravo, which was about a two hour car trip from our home in the hills above Mexico City. This beautiful Mexican town is situated in a forest, surrounded by a pristine aqua lake. Many people compare it to a Swiss Village. We didn't even know that this house existed for over a year.

One day the Mistress returned from a trip to the United States with two cat carriers. She opened them up in our favorite sunning room, and left us alone. Of course our curiosity got the best of us. We sniffed them, gingerly stepped into them, and jumped right out. After several hours of close proximity, we no longer were intimidated. Then the Mistress set our food dishes in these carriers. That act triggered the alarms in our heads, enough to ignore the food. To our surprise, we were offered no other dinner, and eventually had to climb back in and eat out of our cat carriers.

The next weekend, Canica and I were placed into the carriers and driven to this weekend home in the woods. It was our second car trip (the first was when we were adopted and brought home) and we protested with meows and yowls. Since we were placed on the floor, we could not see the beautiful scenery or enjoy the black and gold Monarch butterflies that Miss Cassandra and Miss Ticiana raved about. Finally we arrived and were released from our cages. Like bolts of lightning, we dashed under the house, where we stayed all night. Miss Cassandra and Miss Ticiana tried to coax us out, worrying that the owls or coyotes would get us, but the adults assured them that we would be fine.

The following morning, awakened by the roosters, we stretched, yawned and crawled out from under the house. What beauty surrounded us! We were sitting

in a clearing in the forest. The sun glimmered off our red tile roof and warmed our coats. We sniffed sweet odors of pine trees, fresh grass and warm earth. The colors were rich and the morning was sparkling. We smelled and then saw smoke coming from our stone fireplace. As we gazed appreciatively at the lovely house, with its tile, stone and thatched foundation, the Mistress called to us from the kitchen. With high expectations, we raced up the wooden steps and through the doorway. This was worth the trip!

After breakfast, Miss Cassandra and Miss Ticiana put the rabbit leashes on us and tried to take us for walks. We balked at this, sat right down

and refused to budge. Gently, they removed the leashes and quietly coaxed us into following them around the yard. With their guidance, we became acquainted with our weekend home. Soon we were following them down to the stream which flowed into a small waterfall. We watched as the girls splashed and played in the water, catching frogs and water puppies. There we discovered large flat rocks which provided warmth for afternoon naps.

Canica and I were now adolescents and curious about everything within our world. Here in Valle de Bravo we reveled in new terrain to explore, and a fantastic house with so many nooks and crannies. In the basement we discovered a family of mice. Early one evening I caught a small one and proudly carried it to Miss Cassandra, who was playing a game with her dad by the fire. She let out a shriek as I gently deposited it by her feet, causing the mouse to run for safety and Miss Cassandra to flee screaming to the kitchen. Puzzled by the reaction, Canica and I decided that perhaps they would prefer these offerings dead. But when he took one to the Mistress, reading in her bed, he got the same reaction. Alas, we no longer took them these valued prizes.

There was a farmer and his family who lived in a

small house on our property and watched over the house while we were gone. One fine day, Canica and I were sleeping in the sun when we heard festive shouts of "Ole!" We stretched and walked to the window, where we witnessed a most unusual sight. The caretaker was dancing about in the street before our house, holding in front of him a red cape, and swaying it back and forth to attract a calf. This young bull was snorting and pawing the ground and quite offended with the ceremony. Suddenly he decided to rush at the cape, which seemed to be the man's intention. More shouts of "Ole" came forth, as the wife and friends joined in. Canica and I were privy to a private bull fight!

As the family realized that we enjoyed our weekend home, they took us more often. We still protested the cat carriers, and often convinced the girls to let us be free in the back seat. The family was a happy lot, and sang songs or played counting games to make the time fly. One song in particular will always remain in my memory. They called it "The Bumpedy Road." It was a parody of one the Mistress's family had invented when she traveled to her childhood weekend cabin. The original song was written because the road was unpaved and bumpy.

My Mistress, her sisters and brothers and their parents, used to ride in an old pick-up truck over this road, bumping all the way. She told us the story many times, laughing at her memories. This old cabin sat next to the Millicoma River, so after they arrived, covered with dust, they would rush down to the river for a swim. Then they all had to clean the cabin of mouse droppings before settling in for the weekend.

The words "It's the Millicoma view" were changed to "It's a Valle de Bravo view." They would always sing this song as we came around the final bend on the outskirts of the town. Everyone would join in the song, even their American childhood friends and

family (remembering it from earlier days) who came to visit us. Here is the song:

*"Now we're on the bumpedy road*
*The bumpedy road, you see . . .*
*Oh we will slip and slide and we'll bounce around the car*
*And soon we'll come to our kitties' bar.*
*Next King's Ranch will come into view*
*A great herd of elk we'll see.*
*It's the Valle de Bravo view*
*You should really see it too*
*It's the cabin life for me!"*

This would be accompanied by many giggles and teasing, since some of them were pretty much tone deaf and sang off key. But everyone had fun, and we quickly learned the words, and sang in our minds. And we were quiet for those few minutes of every trip, because we cats do like singing.

# Guardian Angels

Canica and I talked about the changes we began to notice in our young ladies. Miss Cassandra was becoming moody, and didn't play outdoors as much as before. She spoke for long periods of time on the telephone, and sometimes seemed irritated and upset. I would go and comfort her by sitting on her lap, licking her hands and reaching up to groom her face with my tongue. She was always gentle with me, but I saw her snap at and argue with her mother and father, and even with Miss Ticiana. Later, while curled up in the family room, I listened to a television program about the ways of teenagers, and decided that was the explanation.

We watched Miss Ticiana too, and found less to worry about. She was still a happy-go-lucky child, but Miss Cassandra's moods affected her as well. Miss Ticiana would sometimes withdraw to the family room, taking only Canica and me and closing the door. We would snuggle with her on the sofa while she watched television, but at times her mind seemed far away. We continued to seek both girls out and stayed close by, just in case they needed to hug someone.

Canica had become quite the handsome dude. His coat was thick and shiny, his body hard and muscular, and he was very much the dandy. Other cats in the neighborhood commented enviously among themselves about his fine appearance. I was still small, and only nominally attractive. I was also much more shy than he, and generally followed his lead. But when it came to our young ladies and their needs, he sought my advice. I explained to Canica that they were growing up into young ladies and, although they still loved and needed us, they also had many other interests. We cats learn from our observational skills. From eavesdropping and watching television, I shared this new information with him. We made a good team, but as the months rolled on, I noticed that he, too, seemed restless, and I wondered if our little world wasn't becoming too confining for Canica.

The girls spent their weekdays in school, and then the Mistress took them to gym and dance classes, school activities, piano lessons, or whatever event was happening. But when they arrived home late afternoon or early evening, we rushed to greet them at the door. They delighted in this show of affection, squealing with pleasure and scooping us up into their arms. We hovered close beside them as they changed clothes, had supper, did homework, and finally bathed and relaxed with their books or television shows. When they retired for the night, we hopped into their beds too. Canica cuddled in Miss Ticiana's arms, and I nestled at the bottom of Miss Cassandra's bed, under the covers, until they fell asleep. Later, cautiously and silently, we opened the bedroom door with our noses and paws, and returned to the rest of the house to make sure we were not missing anything exciting.

Señorita Teresa might be cleaning up the kitchen and we could find delicious dinner bits awaiting us in our dishes. Perhaps the Master and Mistress were entertaining, so we could curl up in a corner and eavesdrop on their conversations, or rub against an unsuspecting guest's leg. The laundry room window was normally left ajar for us, so we could go into the night and explore.

Our neighborhood was rife for adventure after 8:00 p.m. We often gathered with the other cats for chats, games or explorations. It was during these night outings that we heard tall tales and exaggerations. Canica even began to flirt with the young females, and often stayed out much later than I. But always, when we were ready, we jumped back through the window and into our warm house. When the girls awoke each morning, Canica and I were there to greet them.

# An End,
# and a Beginning

The first notes of sadness entered our lives at the beginning of our third year with the family. The Mistress and Master were arguing often, mostly at night when they thought the young ladies were asleep. When this occurred, Canica and I stayed close to the girls, purring loudly to muffle the angry voices. As they whispered anxiously across their beds, we attempted to distract them with silly antics like chasing our tails or softly biting their fingers. Then they would hold us close and whisper to us how confused they felt. They wanted their parents to be happy, and told us they didn't know what to do to help them. Our poor girls.

One day the Master moved out of our house to his own apartment in the city. All of us were very sad. Canica and I did our best to comfort the girls, as well as trying to console the Mistress. The Master often came to our house for the "comida," (the big meal of the day, around two o'clock) and would stay awhile with his daughters, then return to work and his home. This seemed even harder for the girls. Even Señorita Teresa was melancholy. We dreaded a forthcoming change. Canica and I longed to see the girls return to their carefree lives and happiness. We did what we could. We spent as much time with them as they permitted us. Our weekend visits to Valle de Bravo were almost nonexistent now, and we missed them. Cats have an uncanny knowledge of events to come. With heavy hearts, Canica and I knew that our idyllic lifestyle was being threatened.

Canica was beginning to spend more time away from all of us now. He was visibly upset around the dissension, and would run out the door when the voices rose in anger. He confided in me that he had a sweetheart, so he ran to her when things got too un-happy at home. Somehow I couldn't pull myself away from the problems. From within myself I found the strength to soothe my girls, and lick away the tears from my Mistress's cheeks.

It was summertime now and everything was happening so quickly. We eavesdropped from the stairway the afternoon that the Master and the Mistress explained the implications of the word "divorce." Everyone was crying and we felt miserable and unable to make things better. Canica and I called an emergency meeting of the neighborhood cats. Although we cats do not understand all that goes on in the humans' head or heart, we all agreed that we should stay close and comfort them. This we did, while suffering ourselves. We loved our family, and couldn't bear to see them so unhappy. Miss Cassandra acted so brave, feeling the need to shelter Miss Ticiana from the painful truth. At night I would lie in her arms while she shivered from the raw reality.

One day we awoke to discover many of the household goods and old clothing lying outside on tables in the patio. People were buying our belongings. I spent all that day hiding, because these people were strangers and not anxious to discover our charms. Soon after that, a huge truck arrived and all of our familiar objects, large and small, were deposited into it. We were perplexed, and had to search for places to hide, because even the beds were gone. The family seemed to be sleeping elsewhere, but we were left with Señorita Teresa in the empty house. Canica and I anticipated an upcoming departure, so we made our rounds, saying goodbye to our friends. We were as melancholy and distressed as we'd been in a long time. Animals have the ability to suffer deeply, especially when their pain involves their beloved family members. The next morning they returned, packed us into our cat carriers, and drove us away to the airport.

The airport is an antagonistic arena for an animal. It is noisy with an artificial odor, and humans are everywhere, speaking nervously and spending a great deal of time crying and shouting. Our family was sitting in a small area with us in carriers at their feet. The Mistress was quiet and red eyed, trying to console the crying children. The Master was sad and weary, and we cats were meowing in our cages.

Eventually the moment arrived when the "goodbyes" were said and we were carried on the plane with the Mistress, Miss Cassandra and Miss Ticiana. Fortunately, we traveled on top with the humans. I later heard that animals usually go down below with cargo. I imagine that the Mistress had something to say about that, and so we traveled with them. The flight was about four hours long, and I know that Canica wailed miserably the entire time. I also protested for a long while, but my voice grew hoarse. Soon, lulled by the engines, I fell into a fitful slumber.

After what seemed an eternity, the plane landed and the noises abated. We had arrived in Tijuana, Mexico and were about to cross an international border into the country that would be home for the next eight years. We went from plane to automobile, still in our carriers, and continued in this uncomfortable, cooped up state. Some lady named Mimi, who we learned was the Mistress's best friend, picked us up in a van and drove us across the border. There were two young male children in that van, which added to our agony, so we were in quite a turmoil when we finally stopped at Mimi's house in San Diego. Canica and I were dazed and exhausted. Neither of us knew that we were going to live in another country!

## Escape

**W**e arrived at Mimi's house and were carried out to the deck. After a few moments, the Mistress suggested that our carriers be opened, and we be allowed to walk about and familiarize ourselves with these temporary quarters. Miss Ticiana worried that Canica would spook and run off to hide. The Mistress opened my carrier, and I unfolded my legs and tentatively stepped out, stretched, yawned and sat down. That must have been what led the Mistress to believe that we would be fine, and she slowly opened Canica's carrier. As soon as the door opened, Canica became a ball of lightning and flew out, not knowing where he was bound except to get away.

We watched in stunned silence as he leapt off the deck, bolted down the hillside and out of sight. The girls and the Mistress called his name and tried to follow him, but he was too fast for them. I couldn't even think clearly to call him to me, as I had done in the past when he was frightened. Poor Miss Ticiana's face crumbled, and the tears rolled down her cheeks. She was too heartbroken to say a word, and her silence drove her sister to tears. Seeing her daughters sobbing, the Mistress quickly organized a search party. Everyone spent the rest of the afternoon looking for Canica. I was left alone, either forgotten or trusted to stay put. I walked into the house and retreated under the bed in the room where Miss Cassandra's luggage was found, and there I stayed for the rest of the day.

When they returned without Canica, I knew what I had to do. Armed with resolve and a determination to end my family's misery, I crept off into the evening in search of my brother. Walking slowly and unsteadily through dark sections of the foreign neighborhood, and relying on my radar to get me back, I called Canica. I cried out to him and willed him to hear me, to be within an earshot, to answer me. That night I heard coyotes calling, and I was frightened. But my will was stronger than fear or even exhaustion, and eventually I heard his mew. He too had run out of steam, and had to lie down to rest. Through troubled dreams he heard my plaintive cries, and he answered me. I hurried to his voice, and fell upon him, covering him with licks and kisses. Then we curled close together and slept.

Very early the following morning, Canica and I slowly found our way back to that strange house in San Diego. Such a welcome we received! My relief was so complete that I crashed under the bed and slept through the day. Canica, on the other hand, was "King of the Household," and reveled in his festivities. Later on, Miss Cassandra came to me and thanked me again and again. As I licked away her tears, I promised her that I would help her through this transition. Cats can only make promises through mind communications, but I know that Miss Cassandra heard and understood me.

# Starting Over

**M**imi's home was our headquarters, and from there each of us licked our wounds. Mimi kept the Mistress busy, the Mistress encouraged the girls to go out and enjoy the summer days, and Canica and I pretty well stayed secluded. We ventured out at night, and tenuously assessed the area. As we heard we'd only be here several days, we felt no need to make friends or establish a routine. Mimi's sons basically ignored us, but the girls continued to look for us every night as they went to bed, and we looked for them.

Soon we settled into a large home in La Costa, a small community in northern San Diego County. Several days after moving in, Miss Ticiana started school. Each morning the Mistress would walk her to the bus stop, and would meet her again in the afternoon. Some days Miss Ticiana would enter the house crying and complaining. She said that her English wasn't good enough. She couldn't understand what the teacher was explaining. Miss Cassandra and my Mistress consoled and encouraged her. Those first days were miserable.

We all constantly battled culture shock. Canica missed his girlfriend, I missed Señorita Teresa and the Master, the girls missed everybody and their Mexican life. The Mistress was busy helping us and setting up a new household. Those first weeks were stressful, but we had each other. And we were all thankful that we had Canica back.

In the fall, Miss Cassandra entered junior high school and the Mistress realized that she would have to find a job. She quickly found part time work, and would leave the house while I was still sleeping to do "marketing jobs" with an employment agency during that fall, winter and spring. Canica and I would often spend entire days alone in the backyard. Other cats strolled by, and we shared the warm cover of the hot tub with them. We began to enjoy our new environment, and watched as the girls slowly became accustomed to their new world. The girls seemed to adapt more quickly to their new country than their mother, who was raised in the United States!

All sorts of dry, crunchy cat food appeared in our bowls after arriving in California. Most of it was flavorful, but sometimes we received "fair to unworthy" food, which called for special actions. When fair food was presented, I would approach it, making sure the Mistress was observing. I would then crouch, leave my tail behind me stretched out on the floor, and sniff. Very slowly I would take two bites, then stand,

shake first my right paw, then my entire body, and walk away, switching my tail as I retreated. When the food was unworthy, I simply approached it, ears and whiskers swept backwards in loathing. I next pretended to scratch loose earth over it. After this burial gesture, I quickly walked away. But, when the Mistress presented me with delicious culinary tidbits, I would reward her good deeds. I settled down in a crouching position, curling my tail around my body, and took my first mouthful. I then began to eat everything without moving a muscle. I must tell you that the Mistress is a fast learner. We were soon enjoying delicious dry and sometimes moist cat foods. However, we both missed the wonderful natural food combinations that Señorita Teresa gave us in Mexico.

The Mistress had been an actress in Mexico, and had several good actor friends in Los Angeles. From time to time, they would drive down to visit her. One day I heard one of them ask her why she didn't continue that acting career in Los Angeles. She replied that Los Angeles was not a good place for a single woman to raise her daughters (nor her cats!) Often these friends recounted interesting tales of the acting world. I noticed that Canica paid close regard to these stories, especially any mention of animal actors.

He later told me that one of our guests was an "animal trainer", who works as an agent for animals to get into commercials and movies. I noticed that he lavished more attention on this actor friend, rubbing against his legs and jumping heavily into his lap, purring and smiling. He told me that he envisioned himself basking in the sun in Los Angeles, working on movie sets and enjoying all the attention and perks. I listened only halfheartedly, amused at his dreams. My dreams were also beginning to blossom with the spring flowers. All the neighborhood cats met at the school yard after dark, and there were several handsome young males that I fancied, but one in particular.

His name was Jesse, and he lived right behind the grade school. Jesse was a marmalade tabby cat, and kept himself very well groomed indeed. He lived with an old couple who adored him, so he was quite used to being spoiled. He liked to listen to our adventures in Mexico, and was so amused that we were bilingual and bicultural. We taught him cat "Spanish," and he taught us songs. Yes, we cats do sing, and it was a new experience for Canica and me. Jesse became my protector, taking me on adventures on the hills, and I believe that Canica almost got his nose out of joint! And the day I got stuck high up on the tree limb, it was Jesse who heard my cries and came up to show me the way back down.

San Diego's weather was so similar to Mexico's that we had no problem adapting. After a year in the new house, the Mistress was advised that it would be sold. So another house had to be found, and we went through the big move once again. Fortunately this time it was only six blocks away, so Canica and I suffered only moments in the cat carrier, and spent just one day under a bed in the new house. At least all the furniture had a familiar smell.

The new house had three levels, a back yard that sided with the next door neighbors, vegetable gardens to play in, and a black cat named Midnight. This cat was very young, very precocious, and extremely pesky. However, he was the nearest cat around and we learned to adjust to each other. Canica and I had the total run of the neighborhood here, and invited our old gang to visit us in the new neighborhood. Dogs were kept on leashes or fenced in, so we felt very safe.

The girls had many friends now, and we were pleased at their development. The Mistress was working as a part time tour director for a Los Angeles travel agency, in addition to her marketing jobs, so everyone seemed to be on track. Life had once again settled down for the family, and for this I was grateful.

## Baths and Catnip

For some inexplicable reason, most humans do not feel that a cat is capable of cleansing himself sufficiently. So, they determine that they must bathe the cat. Both Canica and I underwent this humiliation a few times in Mexico, but the family seemed to find it more fitting when we moved to California. Perhaps this was because California was such an outdoors kind of place, and all of us spent so much time in the fresh air. Bathing was a mortifying experience at any time, but I learned to complain less as the years went by, perhaps hoping for a quicker release.

Here is the scenario. First I was usually shut in a small room. Then I could hear the Mistress running water in the sink of the laundry room, so I figured out rather quickly that I would soon be in that sink. I was picked up and carried into the bath, drenched with water, smeared with soap, rinsed and soaped and rinsed again, and finally lifted out to be dried in large towels. In the beginning I protested throughout the procedure, but I've learned that submitting meekly evokes pity. Afterwards, we were pampered with delicious morsels or other favors if we behaved. So now I let the bathing take its course. After I'm dried off, I'm usually left alone in a sunny room to preen and dry myself. Naturally when I'm allowed to go outside, I immediately roll in warm dirt or freshly cut grass. I really don't understand this peculiarity of human cat lovers, but I've learned to accept it as one of their strange notions.

This brings me to another question: why is it okay for humans to bathe in bathtubs, but not okay for cats to venture in and drink? Every time I sneak in to lap up water from the bathtub's spout, I get into trouble. I really get scolded when I've come in from the outdoors on a rainy day and head for a sip of tap water in the bathtub. It is something about the footprints that bothers them. I've also discovered that it's not okay to shake yourself dry in a living room, or any other room for that matter, after being bathed or coming in out of the rain. Go figure.

Cats are the detectives of the animal kingdom. We are naturally curious. We are always sniffing around, sneaking into small areas, digging about in imaginary holes, and scratching wherever we like. We love to squeeze our bodies into tiny spaces, and when confused, we resort to digging. Our curiosity has led us into untold adventures, and that is our excuse when we are discovered to be culprits. Once I had to lead Miss Ticiana to a dresser drawer, into which Canica had crawled when it was open. After someone shut it, he couldn't get out, and although he was content for several hours he soon became hungry. Then he called to me to free him. After trying unsuccessfully to paw it open, I brought Miss Ticiana to his aid. This became a favorite story!

Most cats will be presented with catnip at least once during their life spans. I was introduced to this plant in Mexico, when Canica and I were given a catnip mouse for Christmas. We responded to it as most cats do: total silliness. Occasionally the Mistress would bring some home for me during my years in California, and I would react basically in the same mode. Sometimes I felt dizzy, but elated. I would feel

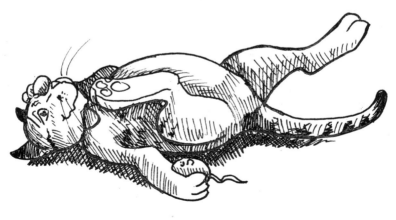

that I just had to lie down on my back and roll. With my four feet in the air and my soft tummy exposed, I would open and close my starfish paws and watch them as if mesmerized. From there, I would roll totally to one side and then roll back to the other side. I would hoist myself to a sitting position and return to the catnip once more.

Suddenly I would realize that I was just too full of energy to keep quiet, so I would have to race around the room, then up the stairs to the bedroom where I would leap onto the bed! There I would stand, lashing my tail with blazing eyes. For the life of me I probably could not have uttered a sound upon command. Does this have something to do with the expression "Has the cat got your tongue?"

# Finding His "Niche"

**W**e had been living the United States a year and a half, and we were all becoming very "Americanized." The only Spanish I heard now was in the house, where the girls spoke it constantly to each other, infrequently with their mother, or on the telephone. Then when the Master came to visit us for almost a month during the summer, our household was a noisy, happy Spanish speaking command center once again.

Canica was becoming restless. He told me he needed more challenges in life, more excitement. He wanted to pursue his acting dreams. I knew he loved us, and how difficult leaving Miss Ticiana would be for him. He trusted that I would watch out for her as well as Miss Cassandra. Briefly, I considered accompanying him to follow his fantasies and to stay with him, but my primary loyalties were to the girls. I also had my own special friends right here, and enjoyed my evenings with them. Our dreams were leading us in different directions. Canica finally convinced me that he could reach Los Angeles safely. One of our street buddies was going up there, so they would travel together.

One afternoon in late fall, Canica came to me and told me he was leaving that night. With a heavy heart, I hugged him to me. We both knew he could not say goodbye to the family, but he did spend all evening with them, purring loudly and gazing lovingly into each face. It made me too sad to witness this act of love. I sat quietly in the Mistress's bedroom. Several times she asked me if I was sick. Miss Ticiana asked Canica if he had a girlfriend, since he was so lovey-dovey. Finally, he took leave of our home, promising to get word to me that he was safe and well. Somehow I knew that he would be, but feared that I would never see him again.

For the next week, I suffered more than ever before

81

in my short life. Miss Cassandra and Miss Ticiana were inconsolable, searching everywhere and posting "Lost Cat" signs throughout the neighborhood. The Mistress wept, hugging me tightly while I dried her tears with my rough tongue. They even showed Canica's picture and relayed his information on the local television station, and put an ad in the paper. Hopefully and uncomprehendingly they awaited his return. It almost broke my heart.

Our pain ebbed as time went by. I caught bits and pieces of their conversations, blaming coyotes or a car accident. But I knew, and could not help them. Finally, I took refuge in long walks and the consolation of my cat friends. I was no longer as carefree and fickle as before, but I was growing up. And my dear girls tried to help me overcome my sadness, as I did with them. Deep in my heart, I knew that Canica had found his niche and was happy. That's how I was finally able to overcome my pain.

# 14

## The Coyote
## and the Cat

One day Miss Cassandra told me we were moving again, because the Mistress still hadn't found her full time job. She felt that she and the girls would have to downsize. Our new house was a townhouse with one less bedroom and smaller dining and living areas. But we fit, and I rather liked the layout. The living room opened onto a deck, from which I could jump down to a garden. Right across the street from us was a wonderful golf course, where I spent many hours roaming and hunting with my friends. I could come and go at my leisure, because the glass door leading to the deck was left ajar for me. We also had a swimming pool in the back patio, and many great trees for scratching purposes. This house was my favorite of the three they had chosen in San Diego.

Before we moved to San Diego, I had never seen coyotes or owls. Both were prevalent in this area, and although I came face to face with an owl, I stayed away from coyotes. I knew that both of these animals carried away cats and even dogs, so I was very much aware of them. The only owls I appreciated were the little ones. On the other hand, I actually witnessed a coyote grab a full-grown cat and run with it! This frightful event happened in that golf course close to our house.

It was late at night, or early morning, and I was out exploring. I had discovered a small flock of ducks down near the club house, and was contently observing them. I did not want to pounce on these critters; rather, I was enjoying the smells and feel of the warm wind rustling my fur. Suddenly I felt a stirring in the bushes a few yards away. I froze, not moving, hardly breathing. I saw a tom cat walking away from me, sauntering with a proud aura of nonchalance. If he had seen me, he was unconcerned, or showing off. I watched him disappear, and moments later heard a piercing shriek shatter the quiet of the winter night. Without moving, and in a crouching position, I watched a coyote wrestle with the tom cat between his jaws. The cat's green eyes had become thin hard slits. Lashing his tail, he was shouting his rage and despair as the coyote managed to run a few yards with him in his mouth. The tom cat was moaning in quiet rage, sounding rather like bagpipes preparing for battle. I was feeling sick and very frightened, wishing I did not have such a close view of the activities. All of a sudden, the coyote slightly loosened his hold. In

that second, the cat slipped from his grasp like a wet bar of soap and streaked down through the trees in a blur of movement. The coyote was surprised, and after shaking all over, retreated. I was trembling, hoping the poor tom cat had escaped unhurt. From that day on, I only visited the golf course when accompanied by my buddies.

# 15

## Cats Have Feelings Too

Just a month after we moved into our town-house, the Mistress landed her full time employment with the government. Now she had to leave for three months of training, and the girls traveled up to Oregon to spend part of this time with the relatives. I was left alone for several weeks, and the neighbor's children were paid to come feed me and play with me. To keep from feeling too lonely, sometimes I invited my band of cat friends over for meals. The food they put out in the afternoon was gone the next morning! This astonished the neighbors, but I flattered them with leg rubbing and loud purring. I was very lonely for Miss Cassandra and Miss Ticiana, and greatly missed snuggling with them in warm beds. I yearned for family noises: the Mistress's chatting with me as she cooked, television news programs, phone calls, even arguments between the girls. I had never been left alone for more than a weekend, and I missed my people.

I turned to my feline friends for entertainment. We took long hunting expeditions into the golf course, where we chased the ducks, teased the squirrels, and stalked birds. We caught bugs in the moonlight and released them, only to be hunted again the following day. The outdoor cats taught me how to be nocturnal. We would settle down next to the golf course's pond and watch the dances of the frogs at midnight! They sang out to each other, coaxing the females to join the males on large lily pads, where all would touch their webbed feet in dance-like motions. It was like a slow motion ballet, quite beautiful!

Finally, Miss Cassandra and Miss Ticiana returned. After giving them the cold shoulder for a brief spell, we made up and I was again content. I followed them everywhere, walking round and round them, looking up into their dear human faces. We spent much time together during the next days.

Their father had again arrived from Mexico to live with them while the Mistress finished up her training, so I received my due attention from all. The nostalgic odors of Mexican cooking filled the house, and I was transported back to my younger, carefree days. When school began in early September, the Mistress returned. Life resumed its tranquil, happy course.

I was truly enjoying my life in California. I had become accustomed to being the only cat in the household, and rather relished my pampered status. The neighbor cats and I would sometimes get together on warm lazy afternoons to sun ourselves. Each of us would share highlights of our days, our human families, our thoughts on life. I still yearned for Canica, but it was a selfish longing to have him close. I could only guess that he had found fulfillment in his new life, wherever he was. Deep in my heart, I knew that Canica was happy.

Miss Cassandra and Miss Ticiana were growing up before my eyes. One summer day friends and relatives arrived for a stay, which I knew marked an event, probably another change. Sure enough, Miss Cassandra was graduating from high school, and the family embarked on planning for the festivities. I was left out of the excitement, but Miss Cassandra always searched for me at night. I purred in her arms until she fell asleep. Then I crawled to the bottom of the bed, between the two sheets, where I slept cozily.

One late summer evening, Cassandra carried me to the front deck and explained that she had to go away to college. She promised she would be back, probably in six weeks. Cats do not have a long term time concept, so I accepted her news without anxiety.

Now we were just three females living there. We were fine, but Miss Cassandra's absence was felt. True to her word, she came back for a short visit, and then again stayed for a longer period during Christmas. A new special person also visited us from time to time. Actually, he visited the Mistress, but had to deal with me as well. He had met her when they attended law enforcement school together (as I discovered by eavesdropping.) They seemed very happy during these visits, and I was sorry to see him leave, because the Mistress became so sad. The following year, we began to see him much more often. He had moved to San Diego, and now lived only a mile away. He brought fun and happiness to our home, and appreciated me as well!

Miss Ticiana missed her sister and complained that she needed her own pet. One day she and the

Mistress brought home a hamster. That's a little animal in the rat family, which cannot communicate with anyone and runs around in circles on a wheel. Absolutely useless, and more boring than the rabbits we once had. But Miss Ticiana played with this animal, which she named "Allie," and found it amusing. One day my curiosity got the best of me and I coaxed Allie to the side of the cage. When I had him within hearing distance, I communicated to him that as long as he behaved himself inside his cage, he could live here. But I would not be protecting him from larger

animals or other dangers if he escaped. I guess it worked, because he stayed with us about two years, causing me no trouble at all. When he passed on, Miss Ticiana came home with an aquarium and gold-fish! Ay yi yi!

I could tolerate all those animal distractions, but I was totally shocked and hurt when my dear Miss Cassandra returned from college with another cat named Gachina. She got it at school and brought it home with her for summer break. Although Miss Cassandra took me in her arms and explained that I was her favorite cat, I was jealous and resentful. I really didn't think that Miss Cassandra understood the nature of cats and territory. I could have visited her elsewhere with her new pet and even accepted the situation. But when she brought her to my house, expecting me to share my home and my family with this outsider, that was just too much!

I spent the first week either hissing or spatting at Gachina (who was constantly underfoot), or hunched up in a bundle of self pity, with disapproval in every whisker. When she approached me for play, I snarled and batted at her, lashing and curling and waving my tail for emphasis. It didn't take long for this young cat to learn respect. After a short time had passed, I became tolerant of her, and eventually accepted her as a "visitor." Both girls continued to give me loving attention and slowly my wounded pride was healed. My neighborhood cat friends helped me to accept an important truth. Cats can share their humans' love and affection with others. Miss Cassandra constantly assured me that I was the "queen," and I made it a point to be the only cat to sleep in her bed every night. When Cassandra returned to the University with Gachina we said our "goodbyes," and I almost looked forward to meeting her again.

# A Feline's Grace

The weather in southern California lent itself to bird watching, a favorite game which I played "solo." On occasion, a bird would land on the terrace just outside the living room. I never felt that I had to catch the bird, but my feline instincts would flare up, and I was ready for action. I crouched on the floor, whiskers bristling and held forward, nose slightly trembling, eyes fixated on the bird. Not a muscle of my body moved, and I could feel electric currents running up my spine. Now my hindquarters began to shake and shiver, my tail lashed back and forth, and suddenly, I was airborne! If the bird had not lifted in flight, it was mine. My family did not appreciate receiving the bird as a gift, so often I would release it unharmed. Either way, the game was the chase.

Cats are very independent creatures. Left to our own, we will survive, and usually quite well. Seldom do you see a starving cat in the wild. A cat will stay alone for a week with food provided and a litter box nearby. We do not like this because we enjoy human closeness, but we will adapt if left by ourselves.

The presence of a cat is regal. No matter how high or low his pedigree, a feline's grace is imposing. Observe the movements of a cat. Even in stretching, his movements are dance-like. Cats walk as if on air, as if they tiptoe through the clouds. The walking of a cat is the ultimate realization of all that is delicate. A poet by the name of Carl Sandburg wrote: "The fog comes on little cat feet." In fact, I've discovered that many poets and writers compare beauty to the cat. I've also heard that there is a musical production called "Cats" in which every character is a human imagining himself into a cat. Miss Cassandra was describing it as lots of cats (people) singing and moving about the stage in cat motions and poses. I would love to see that!

Dogs are fun pets, so I've heard. They do what their masters command. They are trained to obey with rewards. Humans seem to like this. My Mistress tells me that in her work dogs are trained to find drugs. She tells me many interesting stories about Toby, her favorite drug dog, and the adventures they've shared. Drug dogs are rewarded with play: in this case, a tug of war with a rolled up towel. It seems to me that cats would only work for food, and only if they desired. Certainly we are intelligent enough to be trained to find drugs, fruit, bombs, etc. But would we enjoy that?

I think some humans do not realize why we cats love to eavesdrop! So much can be learned by listening to conversations where we have not been invited. I know when my people are going to go away long before the suitcases appear. I've been prepared to hide when I hear that a trip to the vet is imminent. Before the very young nieces and nephews actually arrive, I've planned my escape routes. Also, cats will discover any secret we want to know. Just try keeping the evidence from us if we are interested in finding it out!

# "I Like Little Pussy, Her Coat Is So Warm"

Another year passed by, and now Miss Ticiana was leaving. She had not yet graduated from high school, but wanted to spend a year with her father and study in Mexico. Prior to the packing of suitcases, there were discussions and tears from both the Mistress and Miss Ticiana. But the Mistress knew how important this would be for her daughter, and finally gave it her blessing. Now there were just two females in the house, the Mistress and me.

That year is etched in my memory as a year of "Kiska adoration." Because there were only the two of us in the house, the Mistress spoiled me gloriously. My food improved, which was fortunate, because I had tired of dried and even wet cat food. She would cook calf and chicken livers and then cut them up and serve them over rice, with the juices poured on top. I would also get small pieces of raw chicken, and even chicken hearts just slightly boiled. These delicacies took me back to the days of my youth, when Señorita Teresa would serve us basically what she served the family. I was also given feline vitamins, which are delicious little tidbits designed to keep us healthy. Catnip toys were brought to me from

time to time, and the Mistress spent hours brushing and playing with me. Even though I missed Miss Ticiana, I was receiving much more of the Mistress's free time now.

One evening I was curled up on the couch smelling the delicious aromas of dinner being prepared. The Mistress had the television turned on while she cooked in the next room. I paid little attention to the program, until I heard a familiar sound: a "meow, mew," followed by a low rumbling "brrrrr." My eyes flew open, and there was Canica! He was starring in a cat food commercial. The Mistress must have heard it also, for she came running into the living room shouting "Kiska, look Kiska. There's Canica!" Astounded, we watched Canica strut around the box of cat food, gobble up his portions, and then gently raise one paw and scratch the air. That endearing gesture was meant for me, of that I am certain! He and I often played that game, and he was sharing his performance with me! The Mistress sat next to me, tears sliding down her cheeks and hugging me tightly. I watched silently, filled with emotion—pain coupled with joy. Dear Canica was before me, but I could not reach him. Could he know he had reached us?

The Mistress told me that Canica was probably "discovered" by an agent, just as he had repeatedly told me he would be. She assured me that he was doing what he did best: showing off and adoring the praise. Her words comforted me, and, as time went by, all of us were able to enjoy these commercials and beam with pride over Canica's success. And at last the girls knew that Canica was well and safe. My brother was a movie star!

# 18

## That Unforgettable Summer

**M**iss Ticiana returned from Mexico and we made it through her senior year without mishaps and only goldfish as alternative pets. Toward the end of the spring, I noticed that the Mistress seemed stressed and preoccupied. Being as astute as I am, I began to worry that we were about to undergo another change. Cats are experts in devising surprises of their own, but we resent changes originated by others. I knew I could do nothing but wait and see.

They say that animals take on the personality traits

of their masters. That may have something to do with my next ailment. Perhaps I developed a nervous disorder because the Mistress was so anxious. Whatever the case, I began to lose my fur on one side. When a cat begins to lose fur, it is a very humiliating and terrible thing indeed! The more that fell out, the more I groomed that area, and even more came out in the wash. My dear family combed me and soothed me, but I was ashamed to go out and about and spent a great deal of time sleeping. After several weeks, this problem disappeared, and I resumed my neighborhood rounds.

The year that Miss Ticiana graduated from high school, our house again filled with visitors: family, friends, and small children. Miss Cassandra also returned, and our house resounded with Spanish music, happy voices and much excitement.

One night Miss Cassandra sat with me and told me she was going to get married! Of course I knew Dan, her husband-to-be, and approved of her choice. But how could I bear to have her leave us? I was her cat, and she was my young lady! She explained that I was and always would be her cat, and it hurt her deeply to leave me. Then she asked me if I would stay with the

Mistress, who would soon be alone (after Miss Ticiana left for college.) She promised to visit me and her mom. I realized that Miss Cassandra was asking for my blessing on her new beginning. Was she afraid to be growing up and leaving us? With a gentle touch of my paw to her face, I acknowledged her request.

During the next month, we had a graduation party for Ticiana, a wedding shower for Cassandra, and finally, the actual wedding. I saw many familiar

faces parade through the house. The Master was back, staying nearby with friends. Other relatives from Mexico came up for the occasion, as well as all of the Mistress's family. Uninterrupted naps were no longer the status quo, nor was being fed on time! But even for a cat, there's good to be found in every situation. Miss Ticiana lavished love and attention on me, knowing she was starting off to college in the fall. I appreciated the variety of new laps to explore, posing myself so that my back was presented in a convenient position for petting. Visitors are notorious for offering morsels from their plates, so I tasted food that normally I would not have. Yet my powers of observation told me that this was not all. The Mistress was still on edge and in the planning stages for something else.

The week of the wedding arrived, amid confusion and commotion in our household, with guests and family members scurrying everywhere. But on the day of the wedding a strange calm overcame our household. Miss Cassandra called to me from upstairs that she had something she wanted to show me.

As she descended the stairway with her sister,my heart stopped! My beautiful Miss Cassandra was glorious in her bridal gown! She radiated serenity and joy. How far she had come from the spirited adolescent who picked out her wild kitten. I watched her and felt faint, but my heart swelled with pride and tears brimmed in my eyes. If only Canica could see her now, and his little Miss Ticiana, standing behind her sister, stunning in her flowered bridesmaid dress. I closed my eyes and sent him a mental message:

"My brother, we did well!"

# Epilogue

We left San Diego one July morning , a month after Cassandra's wedding. The Mistress, her boyfriend and I were crammed into her small convertible, en route to Canada, which would become our new home. I did not know then that we would share six splendid years in White Rock, British Columbia. Many changes were awaiting us. Another wedding was forthcoming, another new house, and a lifetime buddy for me were just a few new pieces to add to our life puzzle. I remember awakening on the day of the move thinking "I have attached myself to these people, not to any particular place. Together, we shall proceed onward."

There is a bright new world out there to explore, and we're on our way!

# About the Author

*2009/2008/2006 Georgia Author of the Year* Pamela Bauer Mueller brings valuable messages about relationships, love, loyalty and acceptance to school groups and civic organizations. Ms. Mueller does considerable research before writing her middle reader/young adult novels. All of her titles have been accepted into the Renaissance Accelerated Reading Program.

Pamela has dreamed of introducing her readers to the history of Georgia's Golden Isles since moving to Georgia. She has now written three historical fiction books featuring local characters. Ms. Mueller was the *2006 Georgia Author of the Year-Children's/Young Adult Literature*, as well as a *2008 Mom's Choice Award* winner and a *2006 Independent Publisher Book Awards Finalist/ Multicultural Category* for her first historical novel entitled *Neptune's Honor*.

*An Angry Drum Echoed: Mary Musgrove, Queen of the Creeks*, is based on the true story of a Creek/Englishwoman who became an emissary and interpreter for General Oglethorpe when he landed in Savannah to found the colony of Georgia. Mary smoothed the path to cooperation between the Indians and the colonists, perhaps single-handedly insuring the survival of colonial Georgia. This title received the *2009 Gold Mom's Choice* the *2008 GA Author of the Year Award.*

Ms. Mueller resides on Jekyll Island, Georgia with her husband Michael and two cats. She was raised in Oregon, graduated from Lewis and Clark College in Portland, and worked as a flight attendant for Pan American Airlines before moving to Mexico City. There she taught English, modeled and acted for 18 years. After returning to the United States, Pamela worked for 12 years as a U.S. Customs Inspector. She served 6 years in San Diego and then was selected for a foreign assignment in Vancouver, British Columbia, Canada.

Ms. Bauer Mueller took an early retirement from the U.S. Customs Service to become a full-time author. She and her Mexican cat, Kiska, wrote *The Kiska Trilogy: The Bumpedy Road, Rain City Cats* and *Eight Paws to Georgia*, which encompassed their adventurous living in Mexico, Canada and the United States. Several years ago, Pamela's daughter raised a guide dog puppy. Pamela eventually depicted this sweet love journey in *Hello, Goodbye, I Love You: The Story of Aloha, A Guide Dog for the Blind*, which was later selected as a *2004 Children's Choice Book* and a *2008 Mom's Choice* award. *The sequel is entitled Aloha Crossing* and follows Aloha's life with her blind partner. This title gave Pamela the *2009 GA Author of the Year*, the *2009 Gold Mom's Choice Award* and the *2009*

*IPPY Gold medal for Middle Readers*. Her newest title, *Splendid Isolation*, released in January 2010, is a finalist in the *USA Book News 2010 Best Books* awards in the Biography/Historical category.

# About the Illustrator

Naomi Marie Weiler was born and raised in the beautiful city of Victoria, British Columbia. This is her first book, which she has truly enjoyed illustrating. She is currently studying art at Vancouver's prestigious Emily Carr Institute of Art. Naomi's passions include theater, jazz and all facets of art. She would like to thank Bobby the Bunny and Bandit the Terror for their inspiration.